To L...

The Wild Ones

Gladys Swedak

Love & Blessing
Gladys.

The Wild Ones

Gladys Swedak

Beach Road Press

Published by Gladys Swedak in conjunction with Summer Bay Press and Beach Road Press.

ISBN: 978-0-9780800-3-7
Digital ISBN: 978-0-9780800-4-4

Acknowledgments

I wish to thank Wendy Dewar Hughes and Beach Road Press for the help and understanding in the publication of The Wild Ones. Without her knowledge and wisdom The Wild Ones would still be an item on a bucket list.

Also my partner, Ken Enns, who told me one day there was a computer downstairs and to go and write. I haven't quit since.

Thank you both.

Chapter 1

I looked out onto the deserted field. *Where is everyone? I am too young to be on my own.* Father went to see what was making the noise on the other side of the hill. Mommy and the rest of the herd went with him. The babies and yearlings were told to stay here and hide until they came back. The yearlings followed the herd later. It has been so long. I'm hungry but the other babies and I stay hidden. *Maybe I will call them and we should follow too, but Mom told me to stay where I am. What do I do?* I whinnied, no answer. Wait; there was a quiet reply from behind me that sounded like Rosie.

"Rosie, where are you?" I called back.

"Behind the willow," came the answer. "Where are you?"

"I'm over here behind the bush," I whinnied back. "What should we do? I'm hungry."

"I don't know. I'm hungry too," she called. "Come over here."

From the other direction came another, deeper whinny. It was Baby! He was named Baby because he was the youngest.

"Baby," I whinnied, "come to the willow where Rosie is." I got up unsteadily as I had been in one position for a long time. I felt as I did when I was born, trying to walk for the first time. After a few steps it got easier. Rosie and I were gangly, leggy four-month-olds and Baby was a month younger.

We gathered under the willow, Rosie, Baby and me, then came Cheekie from under another bush. Four of us. Where were the others?

I called again. "Everyone come to the big willow." We waited anxiously while only Star,

Chief, and Blaze came from their various hiding places. We nickered and whinnied.

"Where is everyone? Where is Mom? I'm hungry." The older of four-month-olds tried to munch the sweet sun warmed grass as we had seen the adults do.

"Come try this," we said. "It isn't bad. We can get used to it and there is a lake where the adults drank." Blaze, Star, Rosie, Chief, and I cautiously tried to eat grass. Cheekie and Baby tried but their teeth were not ready to chew grass yet. They kind of gummed it. When we thought we had enough of this stuff we went over to the lake and tried to drink. Again Baby and Cheekie couldn't quite get it.

The sun was going down and we were tired and scared. We had never been alone in the dark before. We lay down together with Baby and Cheekie in the middle. They were scared and whimpering with hunger. We were all scared but did not let them know.

One adult came from the direction the herd had gone, but only one. We all got up and saw it was Old Molly, Baby's mother.

We run to her. "Where are the others?" we asked. "Where are our mothers and father?"

Old Molly answered wearily, "They are all gone. By the time I caught up, others of our kind with men on their backs had already captured our family. The men looked at me, and shook blankets and ropes but I ran away. Where are the rest of the babies?"

As Molly was telling us what had happened, Baby and Cheekie tried to nurse from the old tired mare. She let them nurse for a few minutes while she explained, "We are all that is left of our family. I will do my best to care of you until the boys are old enough. If you only nurse for a short time I will try to give each of you a little nourishment".

"We, the older ones, tried to eat grass and drink water from the lake," I told Molly. "The water is cold though."

"You will have to get used to the cold water but I will give each of you a little warm milk."

Baby and Cheekie had finished nursing and Molly asked the younger of us if they want some. Star and Rosie took what was left. Molly promised Blaze, Chief and me that we would get some in the morning. We all lay down again feeling much better now that Molly was with us. She stood over us with Baby and Cheekie lying close to her.

In the morning we looked for Shrimp, Baldy and Stockings. We found their bodies but wished we hadn't.

Now we knew there is only us, with only Molly to care for us.

Chapter 2

Molly did a good job of caring for her six foster babies and her son. We formed a strong bond. The older foals helped to look after the young ones.

We had been a family for about a year when Molly left, telling us, "Do not follow me this time. You older foals look after the young ones. I love you all. Good-bye."

We didn't know what she meant but we did as she said since we usually followed her wherever she went. Now we were alone again.

Nickering and whinnying, we waited for Molly to return. Somehow I knew she wouldn't return, by the way she said good-bye, telling us not to follow her.

What are we going to do now? I wondered, *and when should I tell the others she isn't returning. Sooner would be better than later. Then we can decide what to do and who will lead us now.* I called the rest, "Hey, guys, come here. I want to tell you something."

"What is it?" Blaze asked. He was the oldest by two days.

"I think Molly isn't coming back," I said, looking at Baby and Cheekie, who were very close to Molly because they had nursed longer than the rest of us. The rest of us always took what milk was left, one at a time, when they were finished.

Baby demanded, "Why did you say that about mother? She loves us and wouldn't leave us alone."

"Baby," I said softly, "I am sorry, but think about the way she said good-bye and how she told us not to follow her. We have always gone with her. She is old and tired. It was a hard job

7

looking after us alone. We haven't always been good. Yes, she loved us; that is what kept her going as long as she did."

Blaze said, "Angel is right. We're on our own now. We must decide what we are going to do and who is going to lead us."

Cheekie said, "Blaze and Angel are the oldest and if we all co-operate like the family Molly taught us to be, we can survive on our own."

"Yes," Blaze replied, "Angel and I are the oldest but it is a big responsibility. I do not want to do it alone. I am also sure that Angel doesn't want to either but together and with your help I'm sure we will make it." We all agreed. "We will all chip in and take responsibility," Rosie said.

Star, who had always been shy and didn't usually say much, said with a determination not like her at all, "I think we should stay here in the valley. There is plenty to eat and drink. There are trees for shelter in the winter. We are familiar with the area and know where not to go."

Blaze and I agreed. "For the time being we will stay. It is almost fall and we can take this time to get used to relying on ourselves. No one leave the valley without telling the others where you are going. We do not want to think that you are safe here when you are off somewhere by yourselves." We all agreed that we needed to know where each was, for our security.

Winter came and we survived. When spring arrived a noise was heard from the other side of the ridge.

I remembered the last time that noise was heard. It was when our mothers told us to hide. That was the last time we saw them.

"Don't anyone go over the ridge to investigate," Blaze said. "We will stay here and hide."

Cheekie, the inquisitive member of our small band, said, "I am going to see what it is."

He cantered up the hill as we called out, "No! Don't go, Cheekie. Come back!"

He disappeared over the top. That was the last time we saw him for quite a while.

We decided that this is a good time to leave the valley. Blaze led us out of the only home we had ever known. All we knew was that we wanted to get as far away from that noise as possible.

Chapter 3

On the other side of the hill Cheekie realized he was alone and had made a big mistake. The men on the backs of others like him saw him and raced after him.

One said, "Wow, what a beauty. He looks like that stallion we caught a few years ago."

"Yeah, sure does. Maybe there were others besides that old mare we chased. She was fast but we couldn't scare her into the trap."

"Let's get him!" the first said.

"The boss can call Bill to break him as he did with the other black and grey stallion."

"If we catch him. Look at him run," a third said.

They cornered and roped Cheekie and

dragged him, fighting the rope, to the ranch. It was a long hard pull as the young stallion was strong. They finally got him in a corral with other horses. He was too scared to recognise any of the horses.

Father, now named Willful, recognised his son. He whinnied and went over and nuzzled him, "I'm so glad to see you. You are a handsome young stallion now. I am very proud of you."

"Father, oh Father! Where is Mom?" Cheekie asked, after he recognised his father and rubbed noses with him. "We thought you were gone. Is Mother here? Where are the others?"

"Your mother was here for a while but now she and some of the others are gone," Willful replied. "Its not so bad here. Lots to eat and drink. We do have to carry men on our backs, though. Most of the men treat us well. I admit it was scary at first but we got used to it. How many are left of our family?

"Six, now that I am here. Blaze, Angel, Baby,

Rosie, Star and Chief. Molly came back and looked after us," Cheekie said.

Willful said with pride, "I knew she would when the men chased her and she got away. She had the knowledge to look after you. How did she manage to nurse all of you?"

Cheekie told his father everything; from the time Angel called everyone together to when Molly left and how they had stayed in the valley.

"Angel told us to hide when we heard the noise today but I had to see what it was. Now I am with you, Father. I missed you. Now I will miss my brothers and sisters."

In the ranch house office, Andy, the foreman, said to the boss, "Remember, when we caught that band of wild horses a few years ago? I am sure today we got another of the band. We saw a three-year old coming over the ridge. He was the spit and image of

Willful. Maybe there are more over there. Tomorrow I'll send Bob and Salty to check out the valley."

The boss and owner of the Circle Bar X Ranch, Norman Wright said, "Sounds like a good idea. There weren't any babies with the band we caught that year. Maybe they were in White Buffalo Valley all the time."

Andy asked, "Boss, can we call Bill again to come and break this one? He did such a good job with Willful. He has that special touch with the wild ones."

Thoughtful, Norman replied, "Yes, I'll call him tomorrow."

Andy said, "'Night, Boss," then left the ranch house and walked past Willful and his son rubbing noses. He went into the bunkhouse where he said to Bob and Salty, "I want you two to go over the ridge into White Buffalo Valley tomorrow. Look for any two- or three-year-olds or signs of a herd being there and what size it might be. Start early and take time to make a good search of the whole valley." Then he went to his own quarters.

Bob said, "I wonder why we have never been over that ridge before?"

Salty wondered the same thing. "Well, we are going tomorrow. We will give it a good looking over."

In the morning, after breakfast, Salty and Bob went out to saddle their horses. On seeing Cheekie they exchanged looks that were both admiring and puzzling. That wild thing they dragged in yesterday, fighting all the way, looked much less frightened today.

"Do you think it's because of Willful that he calmed down?" Salty asked.

"I really don't know, Salty," Bob replied. "Maybe seeing Willful helped calm him down. They do look alike. There is no doubt they are sire and son. Well, let's go see what we can find on the other side of the ridge."

They mounted their horses and rode towards the ridge and, for the first time, into White Buffalo Valley. As far as they knew, no one had been in this valley, at least since they came to the ranch three years before. When they got down into the valley they could see a small herd had been there.

"Maybe the herd is still here," Bob said. "Let's look around."

They dismounted and went in opposite directions. "Bob," Salty called after a few minutes. "Come here. What do you make of these skeletons?"

"From the size of them they look like very young animals," Bob said. "Maybe the young ones left when we rounded up that herd. We should have come over and looked. I wonder if that old mare came back and cared for the babies. It would have been a big job for her if she had."

They continued looking for signs and saw that a small herd of young horses had been there. Hoof prints went out of the valley but did not return.

"When that colt came over the ridge, the others must have run in the opposite direction as fast as they could," Salty said.

It was still early so they decided to follow the tracks for a while. Beginning to be able to recognise the prints, they counted the number of horses.

"Looks like six of them," Salty said as he watched the ground. "Young and strong by the stride."

"Yeah," Bob said, "they slowed down, taking time to nibble grass and drink. I think it is time to return and make our report to the boss. We may find out why no one has ever been over here before."

They rode back to the ranch in relative silence, both thinking about the small band of young horses that had recently left the valley. White Buffalo Valley, shaped like a large bowl with a crystal clear pool in the centre, had only the one entrance, and other than over the high ridge that faced the ranch, was secure. One of the three ridges was in the shape of a huge Buffalo and when covered with snow looked like a White Buffalo, which gave the valley its name.

At the ranch the two cowboys gave their report to Andy and the boss. "A small, young band of six or seven horses left the valley recently."

Chapter 4

We ran until we grew tired then slowed down.
Blaze and I kept checking behind us. No one
followed. We arrived in an area unknown to us
and scouted around. There was plenty to eat and
drink, sweet grass and a stream. There were a
few other animals but nothing to frighten us. We
decided to stay a while. Now we were out of our
valley, we had wanderlust to see more of this big
world. Rosie and Baby went into a canyon to
explore and found it a box canyon with no exit
and came back and tell us. "We have to
remember not to run into that canyon if we are
chased. There is no way out."

Star and Chief had gone down another way
and found a clearing with an escape route if we

needed it.

Blaze, Chief and Baby began to feel and look at us differently. Rosie and Star had come to tell me the boys wouldn't let them do things they had done since they were babies. Baby wouldn't let Rosie lead when they explored. Chief wouldn't let Star play with him as they used to. Blaze stopped confiding in me. It was Chief he confided in now. They made the decisions then told the rest of us. Something had changed but I was not sure what. I noticed I felt different, too.

The sound of galloping hooves came from the open canyon and suddenly into the valley charged a large herd led by a golden mare and followed by a big white stallion. He stopped, reared high on his hind legs and glared at us, screamed a challenge to Blaze, Chief and Baby. They looked at him in wonder and nickered a warm greeting. Why had he challenged them? All we wanted was to live here in peace and maybe be a part of his big family. Suddenly, he charged Blaze with teeth bared and let out a whoosh of pent up air from his lungs. His eyes flashed, wide with anger. Blaze sidestepped and just missed the flashing teeth and slashing hooves. He realized he had to fight for his life and ours. Unsure of what to do, he called Chief and Baby to help him. The white stallion was big but unknown to us, he was old and tired. The fight was short and the old stallion backed off and left. Blaze, Chief and Baby didn't have time wonder what had happened.

Coming from the front of the stallion's herd the golden mare whinnied angrily, "Now look what you've done," she snorted. "What are you going to do now, you young whippersnappers? Have any idea what you just did?"

Feeling his power, Blaze stretched his neck high. "Defending myself and my family! He came at me in a rage. I had to defend us."

She ignored the big black and grey stallion and continued, "What you just did was defeat the leader of our herd. He was a good and strong stallion. It took three of you to scare him off. That means one of you is our leader. I am sure you three will fight for supremacy.

"No way will I fight Blaze," Chief said.

Baby said quietly, as he stepped back, "I have always followed Blaze and Chief. I am no leader nor do I want to be."

"Where is the rest of your herd?" the mare asked looking at the six of us.

"We are all there is!" I shouted. This mare had no right to question Blaze or any of us. "The rest are gone. We have been on our own except for an old mare since we were four months old."

"What to you mean, you were on your own?" the mare asked. "Where is the rest of your herd?"

"Gone, I told you," I reply.

"Gone where; how?" she asked, less harshly now.

Between us we told her what happened, right from the time we were hidden by our mothers.

"Oh, I am sorry about that," she said, "but

that doesn't change the fact that one of the stallions will be our leader."

"What about me?" I asked angrily. "It was decided a long time ago that Blaze and I would lead together. It seems I have been forgotten and Chief took my place."

The mare said with kindness, "You are only a mare and can only follow where the leader takes us. You have no say except about the colts and fillies. The oldest mare, me, may if asked, assist and support the leader but only the oldest and little one, I am much older than you. So it will be me who assists the leader. Baby will have to go off on his own and maybe Chief or Blaze, depending on who is going to be the leader. But Baby will have to go for sure."

Blaze, who had had enough of this mare, snorted angrily, "Look Lady! This is my family and where I go they go or we stay on our own. Do you understand? Either we all stay or we all go"

"But," the mare that Blaze had just called Lady

said, "there is only one leader with a herd of mares and foals. All males leave when they reach the age of puberty."

"Not in my family." Blaze said with determination. "If Chief and Baby go, I go, and Angel, Star and Rosie as well."

"Okay, okay, have it your own way," Lady said knowingly, "but you will see and I hope it isn't too late when you do."

"But, um...um Lady," Blaze said with trepidation and fear in his voice, "What do I do now? I have no idea how to be a leader. We were seven and now six since we were babies. If I have to do this will you show me how?"

I was getting angry from being ignored. I was, until a few weeks before, a partner with Blaze. "What about me?" I asked again, and stomped my right front foot, "and Rosie, Star, Chief and Baby? We are a part of this family aren't we? Why are you both ignoring us?"

Rosie whinnied, "Leave Star and me out of

24

this. We have no interest in being anything but a part of a family. If Lady will tell us what is expected of us we will do it."

Lady replied, "The only thing expected of you is to follow and care for the young. Protect them."

"Like Molly did for us," Rosie said.

"Yes, I suppose so," Lady said, "Now, go over with the rest of the herd and get acquainted. They are all quite nice."

Rosie and Star wandered over to where the herd was milling about munching grass, as they tried to pretend not to watch what was going on. They knew they had a new leader.

I was not moving from the spot I had rooted myself to. I wanted some answers before I just become another mare amongst all the others.

"Blaze," I whined, "What is going to happen to our little family? Are we going to be as close or are Rosie, Star and I just to become members of this big herd? Why can't we just go on as we were? We did all right by ourselves. Blaze, please!"

Lady said, demandingly now, "Do as I told you. Go over with the others."

Blaze came to my defence and snorted. "Lady, do not ever talk to any of my family that way or we will do just as she said. I will handle this my way."

"Yes, I understand. You handle it. I will go back to the herd." She looked at me and added, "When you are ready to come I will introduce you to the rest of the mares. We will stay here for a while any way. We usually come here at this time of the year. The babies are about to be born." Then she trotted off like the matriarch she was, towards the grazing mares.

"Angel, please," Blaze pleaded. "Listen to me for a few minutes. We can't continue on our own. We know nothing about what we are feeling, where to go or what to do. There is more protection in a bigger herd than with just the six of us. We need them and since we defeated their leader they need us. Give it a chance please. I know it will be hard for a while but we will all get used to being a part of a bigger family. That's how it would have been if our parents hadn't gone away."

Chief added, "Blaze is right, Angel. Things will be different but maybe better. Give it and us a chance to try and live as one big family. If things don't work out, we will all try to come up with a solution. Okay?"

"Okay, I'll give it a chance, but I am not going to be just one of the crowd," I said and trotted over to where Rosie and Star were getting acquainted with some of the other mares.

Chapter 5

At the ranch, Salty finished his explanation. "We followed them for a ways out of the valley. At first the tracks said they were running fast then they slowed down."

"Have we heard from Bill yet?" Bob asked changing the subject.

"Yes," Andy said, "He's coming in a few days. He told us not to go near that horse until he gets here."

"He always said that," one of the hands replied. "You will see why when he gets here," he told the newer hands.

A few days later an old beat up truck thundered into the yard. "What in the world is that?" one of the new hands asked.

"That is Bill," Andy said, and they went out into the yard. Bill was climbing out of the space where a door window should have been.

"Bill, why don't you trade that heap in for a sensible truck?" Norman asked him.

Bill replied, "Why should I? This one runs just fine."

"Yes, but it scares every living creature within a hundred miles."

"Oh well," Bill said, with a big smile, "they'll get used to it again." He was the kind of man you liked or disliked on sight. He had a face that could hide nothing. His six foot frame demanded respect, but his personality didn't fit it at all. "Where is this horse you want me to see?" he asked.

Salty said, "Wait until you see him, Bill. He is the image of Willful. He is in the corral with Willful."

"Okay, lets go and see him."

Cheekie had calmed down. No one had been near him in the week he had been in the corral with his father. Willful tried his best to tell Cheekie what was going to happen to him.

"You will have men ride you as you have seen others ridden," he told his son, "but first you will be trained."

"What do you mean, Father?" Cheekie asked. "Trained how?"

"Well," Willful said, "A man will come and train you to accept a bridle and saddle then a man on your back. You will have to learn to go where they lead you. It can be hard or easy depending on your attitude."

"No one will ever get on my back!" Cheekie said with determination, and shook his head up and down.

"Oh, but they will, son," Willful replied, remembering how he had fought against that very thing a few years ago. He saw the men coming and recognised Bill as the man who had trained him. *Oh good*, he thought, *now we will see who is right*. He trotted over to the fence as Bill jumped over.

As he walked to the corral, Bill watched the two blacks. *My goodness*, he thought, *another Willful*. He reached up to pat Willful's neck and said, "Hi, Big Boy. Who is this with you? I'll bet you're glad to see him. I think I'll keep him. I wanted you but the boss had other ideas for you. But he won't want two of you." Still looking at and stroking Willful's long, sleek shinny neck, he said to Cheekie, "Hello, Beauty, I'm Bill, and we're going to become friends just like your sire and me." He took an apple out of his pocket and put his hand out. Willful took the apple and munched it. Bill gave Willful a final pat and left the corral. *Our first contact went well,* he thought. *That young black is now curious as to what his father is chewing and where it came from.*

When Cheekie saw Bill came over the fence he trotted to the far side of the corral but still kept his eyes on his father. Why was Father going over to that man and letting him touch him? Sounds were coming from him. What had Father taken from his hand?

Willful, still chewing the remains of the apple came over to where his son was. "Father, what are you chewing?" Cheekie asked. "Why did you let him touch you? Did it hurt?"

Willful swallowed the last of the apple and said, "If you take a breath and let me get a word in, I will tell you. I was chewing something very good and juicy. He was the man who trained me and will be training you. He always has something good to eat in his hand. I let him touch me because it feels good and comforting. No, that man has never hurt me and he will not hurt you either. I promise."

For the next few days Bill came into the corral, patted Willful and give him a treat. All the time he was in the corral with them he was talking to them. He never seemed to pay any attention to Cheekie but was constantly watching him. Sometimes Bill saddled Willful and rode away.

Cheekie was scared when the man took his father away but they always come back. He was also becoming annoyed with this man who his father said was going to be training him. He was ready to fight but there was nothing to fight. After a while he moved slowly closer to where Bill and Willful were. *Not too close mind*, he told himself. *This may be a trap*. He stood shivering, wanting whatever his father had but was afraid, so he just watched Willful chew another treat.

It had been a week since this training began

and Cheekie was just about arms length away now. "Well, Beauty," Bill said, "You didn't take as long as Willful. Want an apple?" Bill slowly held out his hand with an apple on it.

Cheekie looked at the apple. *Father said this round thing was good. Should I try it?* "Father, tell me what to do. I'm scared," he whinnied.

Willful munched on the apple Bill gave him mumbled, "Take it; it's good. I have told you the man will not hurt you. He may touch you but that is all."

Cheekie gingerly put his lips over the apple and bit it. He tried to talk with his mouth full and mumbled, "Oh ye, ish goo."

"Well that was easy," Bill said to Willful. "What did you say to him? Next time I'll try to touch him." He walked away, leaving the two blacks munching on apples.

The watching ranch hands knew this

wasn't going to take as long as it took with Willful, but it would be a while yet. They had watched each step before and knew exactly what was coming.

"Andy," Salty said, "the boss was sure lucky to have found Bill. He is good. He seems to know just what to do to make them come to him."

"Yes, he does," Andy said in reply. "Bill is well known for the job he does with the wild ones. Especially if you have the time to wait and want a well-trained, spirited horse."

Bill had been feeding the horse he called Beauty apples, carrots or sugar lumps for a few days. "Today is the day, Beauty," he said. "I am going to rub your neck just as I do with your father."

Cheekie came over for his treat now just as readily as his father. "Father," he said, "those things the man put on his hand are good. This isn't bad at all."

"Soon he will touch you," Willful said knowingly.

"Will it hurt, Father?" Cheekie asked.

"No it will not hurt," Willful told him once again. "It may feel funny at first but after awhile it is pleasant. Soon you will come to expect and like it."

While they were munching happily Bill put his hand on Willful's neck and rubbed gently. He let Cheekie come to him as he rubbed Willful's neck. He had his hand out close to Cheekie's nose. Cheekie lifted his head and sniffed and blew air, shaking his head. *This has a strange smell,* he thought, *but he is rubbing father's neck.* "What does it feel like, Father?" he asked.

"It feels good, son," Willful said, getting closer to Bill.

"Beauty, Beauty," Bill called softly. "Come Beauty." He didn't move more than an inch closer to the big grey and black horse.

Cheekie, as if knowing that Bill was calling him, came a few steps closer and stretched out his neck as far as it would go, just barely touching Bill's hand with his nose.

Bill did not move. He knew how sensitive this first contact was. It could be the beginning of trust or the beginning of starting all over with getting the animal to come close again. Beauty pulled back only a step then came back, a little nearer. He moved his head ever so slightly so there was movement between his face and Bill's hand.

"Father," he said, "that does feel nice. It

doesn't hurt at all."

Hearing the horses communicate, Bill said quietly, "What is he asking and what are you telling him? This is much easier than with you but you didn't have anyone around to help you understand, did you? Keep up the good work, Willful. I'll see you two tomorrow. That is enough for to day." He left the corral.

Bill went into the house and told Norman what he had discovered about father and son then said, "I would like it if after I've gentled him if I may buy him from you. You don't want two beautiful black studs. Do you? I am also sure you would not want to geld him."

"We will talk about it later," Norman said. He knew just how much Bill loved Willful and wanted him. He did owe Bill something for all the work he had done with Willful and now with Beauty, so maybe he just might let him have Beauty. No, there would be no way he would geld that wild one and there would be no way that they could co-exist here together after Beauty became mature and knew what to do.

Chapter 6

We got used to being members of a large herd. Blaze and Chief shared the responsibilities of being leader.

"This is weird," Lady said one day in late summer. "There have never been two leaders. I hope they know what they are doing."

"You don't understand our family," I told her. "We are so close that there will be no fighting between Blaze and Chief. Baby is a follower not a leader, so why does it bothering you so much? Rosie and Star are mingling with the other mares and I have every intention of getting along with you. I hope you will tell us what is happening to us and explain why Blaze and Chief and Baby are acting so strangely towards us?"

"That is what I am talking about," Lady said, with a knowing grin.

As we wandered over to where Rosie and Star mingled with the other mares, Rosie came to us and said, "Angel, are we really going to stay with the herd? I like being among these mares. They are nice and willing talk to us."

Lady looked at me and said, "Well, go ahead and tell her."

"Yes, Rosie, we are staying, all of us. No one is leaving. Lady has accepted both Blaze and Chief as leaders."

A few days later Lady called us. "Angel, Rosie, Star, come here please. It is time for your education to begin."

I was beginning to respect this old mare. She was so much like Molly. Gentle with us, yet teaching us how to be members of a herd and how to be female.

"What education? You have been teaching us since we got here. We had no idea of how little we know."

"What you are going to learn now," Lady said, "is where babies come from."

"We know," Rosie said, "babies come from their mother."

"Yes," Lady said, "but do you know how they get inside the mother?"

"That's easy," Star said. "Mother Nature put them there."

Lady was amused at that answer but it told her that she had to start at the beginning. "Let's go over here by ourselves. Yes, Mother Nature has a hand in it by making the mare mature so that she is ready to become a mother. The mare will produce a scent, which tells the leader and father that she is ready to receive him. That is what is bothering you and Blaze, Chief and maybe Baby. You have noticed, I am sure, that there is a difference between you and the boys. It is the coming together of the stallion and the mare that produces a baby. The next spring the babies are born. That is why usually only one stallion is with a herd of mares. The jealousy between the males can be violent as you saw when our leader and father thought that Blaze was going to take his family."

"We just wanted to join your family. Blaze didn't want to be the leader," I said in our defense.

"Yes, that is what you thought," Lady said, "but our stallion did not know that and he would not have allowed Blaze, Chief or Baby to join us. You, Rosie and Star, yes, because you are females."

Star, who had been listening closely to all of this said, "I don't want to be a mother. I do not know how to look after myself let alone a baby."

"You'll learn like all of us had to," Lady said. "Now comes the hard job of telling Blaze and Chief what they have to do. It seems they don't know either. You can go back to the herd and mingle with the mothers and watch them."

43

Rosie, Star and I wandered slowly back to the herd and muttered amongst ourselves. "This is all so strange," Rosie said. "I don't think I want to be a mother. Lady makes it seem so simple but I don't think it is."

Star said again, "I don't want to be a mother either. I just will not let Blaze or Baby do that to me. Maybe Chief, though."

While we were discussing whom we would allow to be the father of our babies, Lady went to where Blaze and Chief stood watching the surrounding area. They were discussing the unfamiliar feelings they had. Lady came up quietly and listened.

Blaze said, "Now I understand why that stallion charged me. He thought we were going to steal some or all of his mares. All we wanted was become a part of the band but there was no way that could have happened. We were young and didn't understand."

"What didn't we understand, Blaze?" Baby

asked as he came up from the other side where he had been drinking from a pool.

"We didn't understand that stallion we defeated in that fight," Chief said. "We thought he was after us and we had to defend ourselves and the girls but he was afraid that we would steal his mares."

"That is right," Lady said as she came up to them. "He was protecting us from you. He thought that Blaze was the leader of your small herd and wanted more."

"I am beginning to understand some of how he felt. I am sorry we chased him away. He could have been a great help to us. Help us please, Lady. We are having strange feelings and are arguing more than we ever did."

"You are becoming mature in ways Mother Nature, as the girls called it, intended. You are ready to be sires to the new babies. You will know what to do when the time comes. Now you have to make the decision I was worried about. Who is

45

going to be the sire? You, Blaze," she looked at the oldest of two young stallions, "or Chief? Will the two of you decide to share, which is very unusual? Baby, I am not worried about. He does not seem to be interested in being a leader. Why, I do not know. Maybe it is a good thing. The decision is up to you. Is Chief going to be just a guardian of the band or does he want to be a sire as well? I will leave it up to you two."

Chapter 7

Bill had been feeding Beauty and Willful apples, carrots and sugar for a few months now. Beauty let Bill touch him, run his hand down the length of his body and around his neck.

"It feels funny, Father, but nice at the same time."

He came to trust this man as his father did. Bill had once or twice taken him along when he rode Willful out of the ranch yard. The first time they went, everyone was afraid Beauty would bolt and run to find his brothers and sisters but Bill had decided to try it.

"Beauty," Bill said one morning, "today you are going to feel something entirely different." He put his hand and arm around Beauty's neck. In his hand he had a neckerchief. He was going to tie it and leave it there for a few hours. He knew Beauty had let him encircle his neck with his hands and arms but would he let this neckerchief stay without fighting it? Slowly he laid the kerchief on Beauty's neck and let it hang down the sides. Beauty looked at Bill but did nothing. Bill took one arm from around Beauty's neck and tied a loose knot in the kerchief. He put his hand back on Beauty; he rubbed the glistening black-grey back, and said, "How do you like that?"

Beauty felt something still on his neck but Bill was rubbing his back so he feels safe.

Willful watched his son with interest. He had

gone through this and wondered what Beauty was going to do. Bill patted Beauty's rump, walked over to Willful and said, "How about that, Willful? The first time and it is still there. Remember when you had the neckerchief on the first time. As soon as I left you got it off."

Beauty wondered why it felt as if Bill's arm was still around his neck when he was on the other side of the corral with father. *Oh well, it feels okay*, he thought. He called to his father, "Father, what's on my neck? The man is over with you but it still feels as if his hand is on my neck"

"Well, my son," Willful whinnied, "that is another step in your training. You have something around your neck. Bill put it there when he petted you. It will not hurt you. Let it be and forget about it."

"Okay," Beauty answered, "You are sure it won't hurt me? It hasn't yet." He still wasn't sure what to make of this. *It is loose enough to come off, if I want,* he thought.

Andy and the men were out on the range fixing fences. They came back into the yard and saw Beauty with the kerchief around his neck. Bob said, "Hey, and look at that. Beauty is one step ahead of Willful."

Andy replied, "Beauty seems to be quite happy even with the neckerchief around his neck. Maybe the next step will be just as easy. Bill did say having Willful there seemed to make things easier. The neckerchief may be on for a few days then comes step three in the process. We will have to wait for that. In the meantime let's get cleaned up and eat. I'm starved."

After dinner Andy went into the house and asked the boss, "After the fences are finished, would it be possible go out looking for this band of wild horses we heard so much about? I understand a big white stallion led them but isn't any longer. Now two blacks are leading the herd."

"That sound like a good idea," Norman Wright said. "Take as many men as you think you need. We may as well do the fall round up at the same time. We all can do with a change of scenery. I may even come with you. You can show me where Willful came from when you got him."

"Great. You haven't been on a horse hunt or round up in a long time," Andy said. "Good night, Boss. See you in the morning."

As Andy went to the bunkhouse he passed the corral with Beauty and Willful. "Good night, boys. I will see if I can find your family in a few days." At the bunkhouse he told the men, "As soon as the fences are fixed we're going on the fall round-up and to hunt that band of horses we have heard so much about. 'Night." He went to his quarters.

The fences were finished quicker than

expected and everyone was excited about going on a wild horse hunt. They had all heard about the two black and grey stallions that seemed to be leading this band.

Chapter 8

Fall was coming and Blaze and Chief wondered where they would winter all these mares and colts. "Maybe we should ask Lady," Chief said. "She seems to know all about what we are suppose to do."

"I don't like having to always ask her what to do and when to do it. We are the leaders not her," Blaze replied, a little angry. He calmed down a bit then said, "But maybe you're right." He looked for Lady and found her with the young mothers. "Lady, come here for a minute, please."

Lady came over to where the stallions were and asked, "Yes, what can I do? I was busy."

"Lady, we think we should go somewhere safer for the winter. Where do you usually spend the winter for shelter from the snow and wind with food for the herd? This valley is too open," Blaze said. He still felt inadequate in Lady's presence. She seemed to know everything he did not. "We could go back to the valley where we grew up. There is a lot of shelter and grass and fresh water there."

Lady said, "It was always the leader's place to take us to winter pasture. It usually wasn't too far from here. Where is the valley you are talking about? Is it far?"

Chief came into the conversation and said, "It is about three or four days from here, in that direction." He nodded his head towards the western mountains where the first skiff of snow had started to show.

"Maybe, if you feel it is safe, we should go there. The valley where we spent last winter was not very good. Many of the young and old died of cold or hunger," Lady replied. "Should I tell the others to get ready to move at sunrise? Is that all right with you?"

Both Blaze and Chief nodded their approval. "Do you really think it is a good idea to go back there?" Chief asked.

"Well, we were safe there. What other choice do we have?" Blaze replied. "We know the way and we know the valley. We tell the herd to do as we say because we know the territory. No more having to ask Lady what to do."

The next morning the herd was ready to go back to the valley we were raised in. I was a little apprehensive but Rosie and Star were anxious to get to the home valley again. It took three long days and we saw others of our kind with strange things on their backs going the other way. Blaze and Chief had been very good at hiding us from the men. They told the herd to do exactly what they said and that way we would be fine. Lady was a little miffed at being just one of the mares now because Blaze and Chief did not need her help in taking us home.

"There. Look, over there. That's where we are going," I told the others when I saw the V shaped entrance to the valley were we grew up. Rosie, Star and I raced ahead. We were home.

"See? Isn't it peaceful here?" I asked. "The strange horses do not come here."

"Yes," Lady said, "it is beautiful and the water is clear and good." She took a long cool drink.

Blaze and Chief called us all together. "This is where we are going to spend the winter. There is shelter from the snow and wind and the lake does not freeze to such a depth that you cannot break the ice to drink. The grass is sweet and will last during the winter. There is one very important thing you all must remember. Do not go over the ridge. If you hear a noise, you hide; you do not go investigate! Do you all understand?"

I said, "That is where our parents went and never returned from when we were young."

Blaze told us, "Explore the valley and pick a special place you want to be your own. There is room for all of us."

Star, Rosie and I knew where our spots were; we had hidden in them as babies. We were the first to find the exact spots to call our own. Lady was so much like Molly that we had come to love her as we had Molly.

I called, "Lady, come over here with us. It is the best place in the whole valley."

"What's so special about this part of the valley? It looks the same as the rest of the valley, with trees to provide shade and protection from the snow. This one has a slight hole in the soil."

Rosie said, "Yes, it is safe and protected. No one ever found us. We couldn't even see each other."

While the horses were getting settled in the valley, we didn't know that Norman Wright and the men from the ranch were getting ready to go out on their fall round up and look for us.

"How many of us are going?" Norman asked Andy. "Is Bill coming with Willful?"

"I think he is leaving Willful with Beauty," Andy replied. "We are leaving the younger hands here to look after the stock. I am sure they will be fine for a few days. Besides it gives them a chance to prove they are as good as they say they are."

Salty came up and said, "Boss, we are ready. Which direction are we going this morning?"

"Okay," Norman said, "We'll start to the south and work our way back around. Move out!"

The men rode to the south, each alone with his thoughts.

Norman thought about his late wife. She had always liked going on these round-ups, checking for wild horses and strays. Norman had not been in the valley of the White Buffalo in a long time. The last time was when he had buried his wife and son there. He did not like to go to the valley because of the memories it brought back. The spirit of the White Buffalo, if seen, was a good luck symbol to his late wife and her people. *This may be a good time to go and see the grave on the way back to the ranch,* he thought.

Bob broke into Norman's thoughts with the question. "Are we going into valley to the north of the ranch? Where we suspect Willful's herd came from."

Only the older ranch hands knew of Norman's wife. She had died before most of them came. "Yes, I think we should. It has been a long time since I have been there. I was just thinking that when you spoke," Norman said.

They travelled a long, wide loop around the ranch. They camped at sundown wherever they happened to be and went on the next day. The chuck wagon went on ahead to set up for meals – mostly beans and pork or rice for lunch and barbecued ranch-raised beef and roast vegetables for dinner. Breakfast was always home grown eggs and bacon with coffee. The evenings were spent singing and telling tall tales of past experiences. It was a kind of a working vacation week. They had found a number of strays and only a few small bands of scrub mares with no stallion. They finally came to the entrance of White Buffalo valley.

Andy saw fresh hoof prints. "Hey, Salty, Bob, come here a minute. Norman, look at this."

"Well, I'll be," Salty said. "Looks as if the babies are back with a big herd in tow."

"This must be the herd we have heard so much about. The one with the two leaders," Norman said. "They might still be in there."

"Do we leave them until spring or get them now?" Andy asked Norman.

Norman, who had psyched himself up to go into the valley, said, "Let's go and take a look. If they are still there we can close off the entrance until spring. If they are not here we can leave it as is."

They rode slowly and quietly into the valley. Salty and Bob remembered the ride through this entrance the other way a year ago as they had followed six young horses.

Chapter 9

Blaze, heard the sound of hooves, and whistled the warning, "HIDE NOW!"

Chief, heard the sound too, repeated the warning. "GO NOW! HIDE!"

Baby, Star, Rosie and I ran to our special places. The others, including Lady, continued doing whatever they are doing. When Blaze and Chief realised the rest of the herd was ignoring the warning it is too late to get them. The men were already here. From our hiding places, memories came flooding back, of being alone and hungry and scared. We were much older now, and not alone and not hungry but we were still scared. The mares started to run but it is too late. They had been seen.

Andy said, "Wow, look at the size of this herd! But where's the stallion? He wouldn't leave his family unguarded."

"Unless it was the two orphan stallions. They would," Salty said.

"We don't see them, so they must be hiding. There were many places to hide." Norman said quietly. "Let's leave them until spring."

"Bob, you and Salty go and close that entrance," Andy said.

As Bob and Salty went to close the entrance, Norman said, "Have someone bring hay during the winter and check up on the herd. Do it quietly and try not to scare the stallions too much. They may bolt and then we won't know where they go."

Andy said, "Good idea, boss. We will be repaid ten fold when we sell them."

Bill asked, "Will you want me to break some of this bunch, too. I would like to get the white ones and gentle them. You would get more for them if they were gentled instead of broken."

"Yeah, okay, "Norman said. "You are hired for the summer next year. The others can be broken. Your method is great but takes so much time. We will see which ones you gentle. The white ones for sure and maybe Willful's family."

Salty and Bob came back and said, "The opening is closed. There is no way for them to get out that way now."

"There is time for the men to go back to the ranch before dinner," Norman said. "Cookie has taken the chuck home. I am going to look around for a while. I may even stay the night."

Andy, who knew why Norman wanted to stay, said, "Okay Boss, see you in the morning."

The men returned to the ranch and put the strays in the pasture. They wondered why Norman, who had never mentioned the valley, now wanted to stay there alone, maybe overnight. Salty, the talker of the group said, "Andy, you have been here longer than any of us. What is it about this valley? The Boss has never been interested in the valley before, now all of sudden he wanted to spend the night."

Andy knew Norman's story and now told the men. "Norman's late wife and son are buried there," he said, hoping that would suffice, and started to walk away.

"Hey, wait a minute, Andy," Bob said. "You can't leave it there. When did they die and how? I never knew Norman had a wife and son."

"It is not my place to say," Andy said, "but she died in childbirth. Oh, I guess it was ten years ago now. The baby didn't survive either. His wife was a tiny thing, almost angelic. It happened about two years after they were married. Norman didn't like to go into the valley because it brought back painful memories. That is all you need to know. Let's go in to dinner."

They went into the bunkhouse where Cookie had the dinner set out. "It is nice to be able to cook on a stove again," he said. "Yep, it's a treat to go on trail rides and cook on an open fire but it is nice to come home to a stove. Wash up, you dirty cowboys and come and get it."

"Cookie, did you know the boss had a wife and son who died in childbirth and that they are buried in the valley to the north of here?" Salty asked.

"Yep, I knew Sophie; the light of the boss's life. She talked him into buying this ranch. When she died, his light went out for a long time," Cookie said with a far away look in his eyes. "Now, come and get it before I throw it out."

Chapter 10

Back in the valley, I saw Norman tether his horse and walk slowly to where I was hiding. I was so scared I wanted to run but was frozen with fear and couldn't move. I heard the man talking softly.

"Oh my love, why? I still miss you so very much. The ranch is a huge success. You and our child should be here to enjoy it with me. We now have a beautiful black stud. We captured him just over that ridge with his band a few years ago. Do you remember Bill Johnson, the horse gentler? Yes, of course you would, you brought him to me when we got Fancy. You wanted her gentled and not broken. Well, he gentled Willful. We called him that because he has a will of his own and always wants his own way and, yes, gets it still sometimes. We don't let him know that or he would be the boss, not me. Bill is working on Willful's son, whom he calls Beauty, who is the image of his father. Just like our child would have been the image of us. I saw him you know. I told you that before, didn't I? Just after he was born. He had your black, shining hair and my eyes and mouth. He would have been a handsome man, my dear.

When we rounded up Willful's herd we missed the babies of the band because I told Andy not to come into your valley. They were gone when Salty and Bob came to look for them. We think they are here again with the herd the big white stallion led."

He was quiet for a while and just looked at the spot where I was but he did not see me. I got up slowly, no longer afraid. I seemed to know the man was not a threat. I wandered over to where Rosie and Baby were hiding. The man was still standing under the big tree looking at the spot I had just left.

"Look," I said, "that man just stands there. He did not even see me. I think we are quite safe from him."

"Where are the boys?" Rosie asked.

"Still hiding," Baby said.

I called, "Blaze Chief, Star. Come here. This man does not even see us."

"That man is strange," Chief said. "I walked right past him and he didn't even see me."

Norman did see a movement but his mind was on his wife and son. The shadow seemed to him to be the spirit of the White Buffalo. "You are here," he said softly. "I can feel your presence. Oh my love, I miss you. I am going to sleep here with you tonight." He took a sandwich out of the saddlebag and a thermos of coffee. He ate his merger dinner; he remembered his life with his beautiful Apache wife. Sophie was the daughter of a chief and destined to wed a young brave of the tribe but on one of her trips to town she met Norman Wright and there was no other man for her. She left her family and disgraced herself but marrying a white man.

They were happy, oh, so happy, and when she told him she was going to have a baby, Norman could have ridden a moonbeam to the stars. Then the snowstorm blocked the road to town the night Norman Jr. was born. The doctor could not get to the ranch and Norman could not get into town.

For years he felt guilty. If only he had taken her into town the week before; if only she had never met him then she would still be alive. It was entirely his fault. Finally, he had come to terms with the guilt and carried on with life.

He finished his meal, and wandered

through the valley, looked up at Buffalo Mountain with just a skiff of snow on its back. Then he came back to the grave and lay down. "Sophie," he said, "I can feel the warmth of your body. Goodnight my love."

As he slept, Norman sensed a presence and he dreamt the White Buffalo came and told him that Sophie and his son were with the spirits and would always be with him and watch over him, too.

After we watched the man eat and wander through our valley then lie down on the stop I had left, we went back to munching a dinner of drying grass. Lady had tried to get out of the valley. "It's blocked. Did you know that?" she said, very upset. "We're stuck here now. Why did you bring us here? Where did you go when the men appeared? There was no danger."

Blaze, who had whistled the first warning said,

"We told you to hide but you didn't, so the men blocked the entrance. If you had hid as we told you, the entrance would still be open. Don't blame us. You and the rest disobeyed me. There is another way out but we're not telling you because it may be dangerous. It is there if we need it. Chief and I will share the watch and keep an eye on the man. The next time I tell you to hide, OBEY."

Chief checked the perimeter of the valley. Everything was in order except for the blocked entrance. Blaze went over to where the man slept and looked at him.

Blaze watched the man sleep and knew there is no threat. He wandered over to talk to the man's horse tethered to a fallen branch. "What is your name?" he asked. "Mine is Blaze. That's Chief," he said and nodded to where Chief drank at the pool. "Together we are leaders of this herd."

Norman's horse, who was uncertain how to

answer, nickered, "I do not know my name but the man called me Kinsman."

Blaze asked, "Where does the man come from? Is it from over the ridge?"

Kinsman said, "Yes, my man came from over the hill. He owns the ranch there. A pair of blacks that look almost like you have been brought in at different times. Norman Wright is the man's name. He is a good man. He treats all of the animals with consideration and care."

"That would be my father and brother," Blaze said. "How are they? Are they well? It had been such a long time since we saw either of them. Cheekie is the name of the younger one."

"They are fine." Kinsman said. "They are getting special treatment from a good friend of Norman's. What is it like to be free and on your own? I have never been free; I was born on the ranch. I don't think I could do it."

"Well," Blaze said, "we are not alone. We have a big herd with us. Thanks for the information about our father and brother. I have to go and relieve Chief for a while. Good-bye."

Norman moaned in his sleep and turned over. He dreamt his wife told him the herd around him could be his if he handled it right. He could get the leaders to follow him anywhere if he had Willful with him.

Morning arrived with a warm fall day. Norman rose and untettered his horse and took him over to the lake for a drink. Norman did not have any thing left to eat for his own breakfast but had a little cold coffee, so he drank that and some water from the lake. "That is good water," he said as if to Kinsman. "No wonder those blacks brought the herd back here. There is shelter from the winter wind and snow. Good water and grazing. They are smart."

From a distance Blaze and Chief watched Norman. Blaze told Chief, "I talked to his horse, Kinsman, last night. He said Father and Cheekie were at the ranch he came from, over the ridge. Maybe we should sneak over there and see for ourselves."

Chief replied skeptically, "What is the matter with you? Don't you remember what happens over the ridge? Our mothers and Molly repeatedly told us not to go over the ridge; it isn't safe over there."

"Yes, I remember," Blaze snorted. "But, Kinsman said it isn't all that bad. Father and Cheekie are living a good life at the ranch."

Chief replied, "What do you know about that horse anyway? Are you sure you can trust what he said?"

Blaze replied, "I know what I saw and what I felt about that horse. I am sure I can trust what he said. He seemed happy enough. He told me he couldn't live as we do."

I come up to the knoll just as Blaze and Chief were discussing the man and his horse. "Good morning," I said. "It looks as if they are going to leave. The man had put something on the horse and got on. They were going over the ridge."

Blaze said, "Good morning to you, too. Let's follow at a distance for a while. I want to see what is on the other side of the ridge."

"You can go," Chief said. "I'll stay here and watch the family."

"Can I come?" I asked excitedly. "I have never been over the ridge and have been curious, too."

"Yes, okay, but only if you do exactly as I say, Angel."

"I will. I promise." We took off at a trot, keeping our distance from the man. He went around the lake and up the hill then down the other side. We were close but far enough behind him to escape if he turned around and chased us.

Chapter 11

At the ranch Bill went out to the corral to see Willful and Beauty. "Good morning, boys," he said happily. "Did you miss me?"

Willful and Beauty trotted over. Beauty still had the kerchief around his neck. "Where is our treat?" Willful whinnied.

"Our treats," Beauty whinnied. "You always have treats."

As if he understood what they said, Bill put his hand in his pocket and came out with a couple of apples. He gave each an apple then rubbed both heads and gently took the scarf off Beauty's neck. Just as gently, he slipped a halter over his head. Beauty felt the difference but gave no outward reaction to the halter other than continuing to munch on his apple. Bill put a rope on the halter and slowly walked around the corral. Beauty and Willful followed him. Beauty wasn't sure why he followed but there is a gentle pull on his head so he went. Bill came back to the gate, slid his hand down Beauty's sleek neck and unlatched the rope.

"Well, Beauty" Bill said, "that was easy. Have a good day, boys." He gave each a pat, and went out of the corral and into the barn. There he checked the blanket for tomorrow. He was going to lay it on Beauty's back after rubbing him with it to show him there was nothing to fear from it. As he put it back on the stall Norman came in.

"Hi, Bill," Norman said. "I am now sure that band is the one led by the two stallions. I saw them last night. Well, actually it was this morning I saw them on a knoll as they watched me. There was a black with grey and a more greyish with black. They have Willful's bloodlines. I think one of them and a mare followed me for a while then went back after they reached the top of the ridge. I saw another stallion but he didn't seem to be involved with the leaders. The greyish-black and white mare and two other mares had the same lines and black and grey colouring. Those must have been the orphans. How is Beauty coming, by the way?"

Bill had never heard Norman talk so much at one time without stopping to take a breath, and he wondered what had happened in the time he had spent in White Buffalo Valley. "Beauty is great," he said. "I have the halter on him already. It sure is easy with Willful's help. Tomorrow comes the blanket. We may be finished before the end of the month, a whole month ahead of the time it took to train Willful. It does seem to help having a relative around. I never would have believed it if I hadn't seen it with my own eyes. Maybe if we get his siblings we will prove or disprove my theory."

Norman said as he went out of the barn, "I will be at the corral tomorrow. This is the shortest time you have taken on any horse."

"Yeah, I imagine more of the men will be there, too," Bill said. He finished in the barn and went out to help with the never-ending ranch work.

The next morning was bright and chilly. After breakfast everyone headed for the corral. Bill first went into the barn for the blanket. He brought it out to the corral, put it on the fence then climbed the fence into the corral. Beauty and Willful came over for their treats. Bill gave them each a carrot and said, "Good morning boys."

Willful liked carrots so he munched his slowly but Beauty, hoping for an apple, ate his quickly. "Where is my sweet treat?" he whinnied.

Of course, Bill didn't understand the whinny so he went and took the blanket off the fence and with one-hand waved it toward Willful who just stood there and enjoyed the remains of his carrot. Then Bill waved it at Beauty who jumped back and ran to the far side of the corral.

"Help, Father. HELP!"

"What? What is the matter?" Willful whinnied

back.

"That thing the man has. What is it? I'm frightened. He waved it at me."

"It is nothing. It won't hurt you and after a while he will put it on your back."

"OH, NO! He won't!" Beauty stated, and stomped his right front foot with the determination he had when he first came to the ranch. He forgot how Bill had done exactly what his father said he would up to that point.

Bill, watched and waved the blanket, then said to the men, "Listen, there is some kind of communication between them." He slowly walked toward the two horses and when he reached Willful he rubbed the blanket along his side then took it in his other hand he let Beauty smell it. Ever so slowly, he rubbed it along Beauty's neck.

Beauty looked at Bill and then his father. *This thing doesn't hurt but no way is he going to put it on my back*, he thought.

It took a few minutes but the blanket did go on Beauty's back. He lifted his rump and it was gone. A minute later it was back. He lifted his rump and tossed it off again. This happened a few times then Beauty realised that this was not working. Each time he bucked it off it was back.

Oh well, he thought. *It isn't that bad and besides it is kind of warm. I think I will leave it for a while.*

Bill remembered how long Willful had thrown the blanket off and run bucking to the farthest corner of the coral so he was completely surprised that Beauty had only gently lifted his rump and it slid off. Willful had continued to buck a few more times before he realised it was off.

He said, "Norman, I think I've proved my point. Next comes the saddle but that can wait for tomorrow. If we capture some of the herd in the valley I would like to try gentling some of the siblings with Beauty acting as teacher's aid. It should be interesting."

The rest of the day was spent preparing the ranch for winter. The first of many wagonloads of hay was taken close to the valley with the trapped herd.

Two of the men, who hadn't been on the round up, took the first wagon of hay and oats to the top of the ridge. They had listened to the men from the round up talk about this herd with the two leaders.

As they unloaded the wagon, Ted said, "Chuck, do you think we can sneak close enough to see this pair?"

Chuck replied, "Sure, I would like to try. This seemed to be the most talked about herd of wild horses."

They tied their horses to one of the trees on the ridge and crawled on their bellies closer to the horses. The wind was with them, as it came from the horses to the men. Only if the wind changed, would the horses be able to smell the men.

Blaze and Chief sniffed the air. There was something wrong but they were not sure what. They smelled men, but where? Blaze was about to whistle a warning but about what? He could not make the herd hide when he didn't see or hear anything. They walked around the perimeter of the valley and came almost on top of where Ted and Chuck hid. Now they were sure they could smell men, but where?

"There are definitely men here," Chief

snorted.

"Let's get back to the herd," Blaze said. "Maybe this is a trick and the herd is being attacked. We will tell them to keep a sharp lookout. I do not think we need to hide."

"Yes," Chief said. "This may be a trick. I smell something besides man but I cannot make out what it is."

Ted and Chuck, hidden under the tall dry grass, lay hardly breathing. When the two black-and-greys left, they took a deep breath.

"Wow, they are beauties," Ted whispered, still not sure if the two could hear him. "There are only a couple of others that look anything like them."

Chuck said with wonder, "'Wow,' is right. Let's get back before they come back. Somehow they know we are here." They crawled back to the wagon and headed for the ranch.

Chapter 12

After the smell of man had left the valley, Blaze and I decided tonight would be a good time to sneak onto the ranch and see Father and Cheekie. We followed that man the other day as far as we dared. Now it was time to find out if Kinsman told the truth about Father and Cheekie. Darkness descended on the valley as we left. We went again where we were told many times never to go, and left Chief in charge. Blaze and I went up and over the ridge.

"Angel," Blaze said, "you must do exactly as I say and when I say it."

"I know. I have promised. I just want to see Cheekie for myself. I don't really remember Father. "

Closer and closer we got to the smell of man and animals. I wanted to turn and run home for safety. Blaze kept going and I followed then we saw the fences. Blaze took off and seemed to fly over the first one. I ran but was afraid to leave the ground.

"Go on, Blaze," I said. "I'll wait here for you. I will hide until you come back." The fact that he may never come back did not occurred to me.

Blaze said, "Only wait until dawn. If I am not back by then, go home. You know the way." Then he ran and jumped another fence, leaving me on the far side of the first fence. Later, he told me that he followed the fence into the ranch yard. He listened and looked in every direction, and saw Father and Cheekie in a corral with other horses.

"Cheekie, is that you?" he asked as he went over to the corral, "and is that father with you?"

"Yes, it's me and father," Cheekie said. "What are you doing here? Father, come quick! It's

Blaze."

"Is that really you, Blaze?" Willful asked the tall, good-looking young stallion. "You were so small the last time I saw you."

"Yes, Father, it is me," Blaze answered. "It was a long time ago that you saw me. Did Cheekie tell you about Molly?"

"Yes, he did, son," Father said. "I told him I knew she would look after you if she escaped the men." What happened after Cheekie came here?"

"Well, Father," Blaze started, forgetting to be watchful, "that is a very long story but to make it short, we left the valley after Cheekie went over the ridge and only a while ago came back to winter in the valley. Chief, Baby and I defeated a big white stallion. Chief and I became leaders of a big herd. The lead mare, Lady, has been a big help."

The ruckus the horses made woke up

Andy and Bill. They put on their pants and boots and went out to see what was making all the noise. In the moonlight they saw a black-and-grey on the wrong side of the fence. Just as they are about to call out they realise that Willful and Beauty were still in the corral.

"This is one of the leaders of the herd," Andy said. "What is he doing here?"

"That is a good question," Bill answered.

"One that may never be answered," Andy replied.

What they didn't know was Willful just asked the same question of his son. "Why are you here and how did you find us?"

Blaze answered, "When the man stayed the night in the valley I talked to his horse, that one over there." He looked at Kinsman and nodded his head. "He said you were here so I came to see

91

for myself. Angel came with me but she couldn't jump so she stayed on the other side of the first fence. She sent you her love."

All of a sudden he saw a movement and screamed with a sound that would have awakened anyone within miles. He took off at a gallop, almost flew out of the yard and over the first fence.

Andy and Bill had never seen any horse on the ranch or anywhere else take off so fast or jump over the five-foot high fence with at least a foot to spare.

"Wow!" Andy said, "Did you see that? What was that? A bird, a plane or a super jumper?"

"I think it was a horse who just discovered he liked to jump," Bill replied.

As they approached the corral, others who had heard the scream came out to see what happened.

Bill said, "Look at Willful and Beauty. They seem agitated. Beauty just tried to jump the corral fence and couldn't get his hindquarters off the ground. There was no jump in him at all."

Norman came out of the house. "What in the world was Willful screaming about?"

Andy and Bill look at each other and Andy said, "That wasn't Willful or Beauty. It was one of the orphans."

Bill smiled, "It looked as if he had come to see his father and brother. He was the one who screamed when he saw us move. He took off like a shot and went over that fence as if it was play. He left a foot clearance. Beauty tried but could not get his hind quarters off the ground."

Andy added, "Look at Willful. He seems as agitated as when he came. He ran around the corral as if someone or something was chasing him. Beauty followed him."

Norman said, "I hope we haven't lost all the ground we gained with both of them. I wonder why that orphan came here. I don't understand why he would."

Andy said, "We were just discussing that when one of us must have moved and he saw us and took off."

Salty added, "Maybe it's because we closed the entrance to the valley. He may be looking for another way out and came into the ranch by accident."

Bob said, "That sound fishy, Salty. Why would he jump fences to find a way out of the valley? He would have gone around them, not over them."

"Well," said Norman, "it is something we may never know. I think we should get back to bed. Morning comes very early around here. Maybe Willful and Beauty will calm down if left alone for the night. Good-night or morning, which ever it is."

All the men went back to their beds. Most wondered why a wild stallion would come into a ranch yard unless he was an outlaw planning to steal mares. This one was not an outlaw and was not interested in stealing mares.

Chapter 13

I had heard Blaze scream and wondered if it was for me to run home. I decided to wait a few minutes until I either saw or heard something. Then I heard the sound of one horse and hoped it was Blaze. There he was coming over the last fence. "Blaze," I nicker, "over here."

"Angel," he said, "I am glad to see you waited for me. I talked with Father and Cheekie. They are well and happy. I didn't get much time to talk. Men came out of the buildings. Let's get home. I want to tell the rest."

"I got worried when I heard you scream and I wanted to run," I said. "I waited because I knew you would look for me if I hadn't waited."

"Yes, I would have," Blaze answered.

We cantered back over the ridge and around the pool, home safe. To Chief, Rosie, Baby and Star it seemed we'd been gone a long time. Blaze told them what happened at the ranch and I told them how I felt, waiting in hiding for him to come back.

"Chief," Blaze continued, "I jumped over a couple of fences. It was a thrilling experience. I am going to do more of it even if it is just over a fallen tree or something. I love it. You should try. You just run and lift off the ground and you're flying."

The next day Lady wanted to know what we found and what we saw. "Did you find a way out of the valley? Are there others over the ridge?"

"There is a way out of the valley that way but we are not going to use it during the winter," Blaze said. "There is a ranch over the ridge and our father and brother are there. It would be dangerous for us to try to leave that way."

I reminded Blaze, "Remember the heap of

grass we saw on the top of the ridge. I wonder where it came from. We may have extra food to eat during the winter."

Lady asked, "What grass lying in a heap? How did it get there?"

Blaze said, "I don't know but we tried it and it is good. There is something else there that's good, too."

The valley was not as plentiful as we thought, maybe because now there was a large herd of mares, yearlings and babies. The grass didn't last as long as it used to for us when we were only seven. We were lucky the pile of dry hay had been brought to us. Lady complained about the lack of food and now the pool was frozen over. It seemed we made a mistake coming home.

Two more piles of hay and grain or oats were left. The wagons came almost weekly and it didn't take long until we had become used to seeing the wagon come and leave food for us.

Chapter 14

On the other side of the ridge, Bill and Andy came out of the bunkhouse, Andy to find out what Norman wanted done that day, and Bill to go to the corral. Willful and Beauty seemed calmer again. Bill went into the corral and offered the horses each an apple. Willful took it but Beauty hesitated. Finally, he accepted it, too. They both chewed the apples as Bill patted both horses.

"Well, Willful, it seemed one of your other sons came for a visit. What did you make of that?" He looked at Beauty. "Today we will just try the blanket again to see how you are feeling about things. You were willing to get your apple but would you stand for the saddle?" Bill got the blanket from the fence and laid it on Beauty's back. Beauty lifted his rump and it fell off. He sniffed at it, picked it up with his teeth, shook his head then dropped it. Bill picked it up and put it back on Beauty's back. This time it stayed on and he walked away with the blanket on his back.

Beauty completely forgot about the blanket and asked, "Father, why do you think Blaze came? It was good to see him. I miss him and the others. I am glad to be with you, though.

Willful said, as he finished his apple, "You know what he said. I will try to talk to Kinsman some time and get his side of it."

In the house, Norman gave Andy the orders for the day. "The hay has to be stacked in the sheds and then we need to winterise the barn."

"Okay, Boss," Andy said, "What about Bill and the horses?"

"What do you mean, 'what about Bill and the horses?'"

"Well, I mean, is he going to be here to work with them over the winter or does he have some where else to go?"

"Yes, he is staying," Norman said. "I hired him for the time being. We'll wait and see what conspires between him and Beauty. If what we think will happen, we will use Beauty to help with the others, the same way Willful is helping with him."

The day was spent getting the hay in and winterising the barn. Most of the horses were in the barn at night during the winter. The cattle were brought into the home range close to the ranch yard.

Finally, after what seemed a long time to

him, Bill said, "I want to try the saddle on Beauty today."

Andy said, "Isn't it a bit fast? Willful had the blanket on for about a week before you tried the saddle. Besides Beauty has been a bit upset lately."

"I know," Bill said. "That bothered me too, but he accepted the blanket and the saddle is the next step."

Andy headed for the house while Bill went into the barn for the saddle and blanket.

"Boss," he called as he entered, "Bill is going to put the saddle on Beauty now. Come and watch." Others heard him and came running. There is no way they were going to miss this.

With everyone lined up at the fence; Bill put the saddle on the gate and called Willful and Beauty. "Come, boys, and get your treats."

As they munched their carrots, Bill picked

up the blanket and put it on Beauty. He reached for the saddle and slid it on Beauty's back. Beauty lifted his hindquarters and off slid the saddle and blanket. This putting on and bucking off was repeated a few times then Beauty walked away with the saddle on his back, the cinch and straps hanging down.

When Beauty reached his father he asked, "What's on my back? The warmer thing has become heavier."

"That is what the man sits on son," Willful said. "Next will came the man."

"I told you no one was going to get on my back!" Beauty insisted and raised his hindquarters. Off went the saddle and blanket.

Bill watched to see how long the saddle

would remain on. When it and the blanket flew off he went over and picked them up. "See you tomorrow boys," he said as he left the corral.

The next day was bright and cold. Andy, who was getting orders for the day, said, "That was weird the way, after rubbing noses with Willful yesterday, the saddle came off. Looks like today will be the full treatment."

"I am going to come and watch this one," Norman replied. "Wasn't able to yesterday because of a phone call. Willful has shortened the training time by weeks."

Bill had just came in. "What has taken a much shorter time? Getting the saddle on Beauty? You are right. I think there was some kind of communication between Willful and Beauty that caused him to buck it off yesterday.

"Maybe," Andy said, "but until he went to his father he wasn't bothered by it. We will see what happens today. Should I take Willful out for a run? It has been a while since I have ridden him."

"I think that would be a good idea," Bill said. "See how Beauty is on his own."

"I'll go and saddle him now," Andy said. "Good luck. Wish I could see this but I did watch you with Willful."

Beauty was alone when Bill went to the corral. He called and gave Beauty an apple then put the blanket and saddle on Beauty's back just as he had the day before but this time he reached under Beauty's belly and brought the cinch strap through and pulled it tight. Beauty quivered when he felt the strap going around his belly. Bill also attached the reins to the halter Beauty had had on since that first day. He walked around the corral and Beauty followed. Beauty trembled a little but did not buck. Bill ran his hand down Beauty's sleek neck, still talking to him.

"Well, Beauty, look at you. It must have been something Willful said that made you buck the saddle off. Andy took your father for a run so we could be alone. Let's walk for a while outside the fence. How would you like to go for a run?"

"Norman," he called a little louder, just enough to be heard. "Open the gate, please. We want to go for a ride."

"Are you sure?" Norman asked.

"Yes, I am sure," Bill said, still walking around the corral. "We have to work outside of the corral sometime."

Norman opened the gate. Everyone else sat on the fence, not wanting to be in the way. As Bill led Beauty out of the corral, Beauty seemed to realise there was no longer a barrier but didn't try to run away.

Bill said, "I am going to try to ride him or at least put some weight on the saddle. I know it is early but I want to try."

"Bill, remember you are in the open," Norman said, "and if he runs off we may lose him back to the orphans."

"I know," Bill replied, "but I don't think he will run away. We may go for a run but we will return, I hope. Here goes." He put his left foot in the stirrup and just hung there for a few minutes and held the reins and saddle horn with one hand and the back of the saddle with the other. Then he swung his right leg over the saddle.

Beauty felt the extra weight and did a little quick step. Bill was still with him, he could smell him, so he felt safe. If he looked around he could see him. *WAIT A MINUTE!* he thought, *there is weight is on my back*!

Bill had just swung his leg over and settled in the saddle. Beauty took one high back leg stand but the weight was still there. *I'll run,* he thought.

107

He came down as if driving piles in the ground and took off.

Bill called back to the watching men, "Keep the gate open. Don't waannttttt…"

That was all Norman and the others heard as Beauty took off.

With Bill glued to the saddle, Beauty ran like the wind.

Bill tried to guide him with the reins on his neck. He laid the left rein on the left side of Beauty's neck and they slowly went to the right. Then the right rein on the right side of Beauty's neck he went left. "Well, Beauty," he shouted over the rushing wind, "you are a fast learner. You're one smart horse. Let's slow down." He pulled back gently on the rein.

Yes, gradually, Beauty slowed down. "Ok," Bill said, "let's see if you will turn around and take us home." He used the reins against Beauty's neck and Bill got him to turned around and headed back to the ranch. He patted his neck and said, "Good Boy, good boy, Beauty."

When they reached the ranch yard, Bill saw Norman had left the gate open. "Good," he said. "Right into the corral, Beauty. I think it is time you got a good brushing."

As they entered the corral Norman closed the gate behind them. "Wow," he asked, "that was some take off from a dead stop. What was the ride like?"

"Ride!" Bill said, "Ha… that was no ride. It was flying. Willful was the only other horse I've ridden who was as fast and easy to sit."

Andy and Willful came into the yard to see Beauty being unsaddled. "Did you do it Bill?" Andy asked.

"Yeah, we did it," Bill said. "We just got back."

"Got back? Back from where?" Andy asked. "You didn't take him out of the corral did you?"

"I sure did," Bill replied. "We went for about a mile or two down past the south pasture. It was almost like the first time I rode Willful out of the yard."

"Well, I'll be," Andy said. Both men unsaddled and brushed down the sweating horses while they talked. The rest of the men had went back to work.

When Beauty and Willful were alone, Beauty said, "Father, oh, father, I went for a run. The man was with me but I couldn't see him."

Willful, who enjoyed his run as well, said, "The man was riding you."

"Oh no, Father," Beauty said, "I told you no one would ever ride me."

"Well, son," Willful said, with a knowing

whinny, "he has."

"I did not realise the extra weight was the man. It wasn't so bad."

"That's right, son," Willful said. "You still get to go out for walks or runs."

Beauty said, "Oh Father, I hope we get to go together sometime. We never did get to run together when I was young.

"Maybe sometime, son," Willful replied. "I would sure like that, too."

The snow started to fall hard and stayed on the ground which was something unusual for this time of the year. It didn't usually last when it snowed this early. Finally it quit and the sun shone. Every thing was covered in a blanket of white. The barn, the house and the ground were all covered.

"Bob, Salty," Andy said one morning, "do you think you could take the sleigh with some hay and grain to the Wild Ones?"

"We can sure give it a try," Salty said.

"Yeah, Boss, I want to see those orphans again," Salty added.

They loaded the sleigh with hay and grain, hitched up a couple of draft horses and headed for White Buffalo Valley. It was hard going but with the big horses and the runners instead of wheels it could be done. It took a little longer than usual but the snow with the sunlight shining on it looks like diamonds.

Chapter 15

In the valley, we had already finished the load of hay and grain that had been brought before. It was hard breaking through the deep hard snow to get at the sparse dry grass. The ice on the lake was thicker this year, too.

"Blaze," I asked, "what are we going to do if we can't break the ice for water and food isn't brought to the top of the ridge?"

Blaze was worried but did not let on. "We may have to try to break through with many trying at the same time. We can always eat the snow if we have to. The men have brought food for a couple of months now. Hopefully, they will continue."

The snow made it quieter in the valley where

we have trampled it down but the hard crust made it easy to hear horses coming.

Chief to where we were standing and said, "Blaze, Angel, look. The men come. They put more hay on the hill. We will let the mares and yearlings eat first then we will eat. Angel, you go and tell them."

"Everyone," I called, "come and get it. Food!"

Just as I was calling, I heard the men. "Hey, Wild Ones come and get it." They slowly walked down into the valley and checked the pool for ice and saw it was frozen solid.

"This is going to be a hard winter," Bob said.

"Yeah," Salty said, as he surveyed the herd and the pool. He stepped on the ice to check its thickness then cracked it so it was still easy for the horses to break. "We may have to break the ice for them later."

Bob said, "We will have to remember to bring an axe the next time we come or bring them water to drink."

"Without us these horses would not make it through the winter," Salty replied as they walked back up the ridge.

We are no longer afraid of the men, though we watched them while we eat. We had begun to accept them being around us. The men left us alone when they brought the food then they left.

When they get back to the ranch, Bob called, "Hey, Boss." He told Andy what they found and that many of the mares looked pregnant.

Salty added, "Where is the axe? I think it should be put in the sleigh so it isn't forgotten the next time we go."

"That's a good idea." Andy replied. "Do you think they can break it until then or should someone go out now and break it?"

"No, I think they can manage it for a few days or a week," Salty said. "I stepped on it and it cracked so it should be okay."

Christmas came and went. The ranch looked like a picture postcard with the mountains in the background and the fences covered with blown snow. The ranch buildings were white and glistened like diamonds. Dark animals dotted the sparkling snow in sunlight and in moonlight.

The sleigh continually brought food to us. The axe was used every time to break the ice for us to drink. Periodically a block of salt was brought as a treat. The men had left us alone but if they wanted to harm us there was nowhere to run anyway. Unknown to us, the contact brought with it a form of trust. We came to expect the men with food. Sometimes we thought we saw Father and Cheekie. We called to them and sometimes they would answer. One bright and cold sunny day I said, "The sleigh is coming. There is Cheekie!"

"Cheekie," Blaze called, "come talk to us."

"I'll try," he answered. He headed towards us but the man stopped him. Then the man dropped the reins on Cheekie's neck and he came over to us and we nuzzled each other. We are all together again.

Blaze asked, "How are you and Father? Is he with you? Does that thing hurt? What is that on your back?"

"Blaze, give me a chance to answer," Cheekie said. "No, it does not hurt. The man on my back is very kind and I trust him with my life. Father is fine but not with us today." He looked at me, and asked, "Angel, how are you? It is good to see all of you again. I missed you."

Bill, on Beauty's back, was stunned by what he saw. "Are you going to introduce me to your family, Beauty, or just ignore me?" he asked. "I wish you could. This is really something for the record book. I decided to give you your head when I heard your family call and you answer. Now I am surrounded by seven different beautiful shades of black and grey horses that seem to be communicating. Sorry, Beauty, but it is time to go." He gently touched his heels to Beauty's sides.

"Bye, guys" Beauty said and nuzzled my nose. "I have to go but I will be back soon."

"'Bye, Cheekie," we all called. "We love you.

Give our love to Father. It was nice to see you again. You look great."

"How was it to be with your family again, Beauty?" Bill asked. "Hey guys, did you see that? I just witnessed a conversation between Beauty and his brothers and sisters."

Andy, who had finished emptying the sleigh, said, "Yeah, I watched it. This is a very special band. We may be able to gentle it before spring with Beauty's and Willful's help."

"Let's get back to the ranch and tell the boss," Bill said.

At the ranch Beauty was unsaddled and brushed down then put in the stall next to Willful.

"Oh, Father," he said. "I saw the family today.

They were great. Blaze said to say hello, and Angel did, too. She doesn't remember you but was looking forward to meeting you again when you come out with us. How do you feel now?"

Willful, had been left behind because of what seemed to be a cold, said, "I am feeling much better with the blanket and the warm mash. I want to see them also. I haven't seen any of them since they were babies, except for Blaze, when he came to the ranch."

Andy and Bill told Norman what transpired with Beauty and the Wild Ones. "It was amazing, Boss," Andy said. "I sat on my horse and watched Bill sit there on Beauty while they seemed to have a conversation."

"If Willful is up to it the next time we go out, I would like to took him," Bill said. "Just to see what happens with him and the boys."

"Sounds like a great idea," Norman

agreed. "He seemed better this afternoon than he did this morning."

The next time the food was taken out to the valley, Willful went too.

"Father," Beauty said, "Having you with me is great."

"Yes, son, it is nice to be out again. I do want to see the others," Willful answered.

As the wagon and riders got close to the valley it was almost as if the Wild Ones had heard them and came to meet them at the top of the ridge.

It was a surprise how after a few months of the men bringing us food we began to expect them. I had taken to the one called Salty. I had even let him feed me out of his hand. Some of the things he gave me were sweet and different from anything I had ever eaten before.

We all seemed to be making a close bond with a man. Blaze and Chief were still skeptical of the men but when Norman came they went close to him but not close enough to eat the sweets out of his hand. Rosie, Star and I tried to tell them what the men had was good. They kept saying, "Maybe next time."

I decided that today was the next time for me. "Blaze, come on and try it. It is good. The man will not hurt you. A big stallion like you could fight him off."

"Okay," Blaze said, "just to get you off my back. Chief," he called, "you have to come too if only to keep Angel happy."

All of the men came from the ranch this time. As they appeared over the rise, Bob said, "Here they come. The girls have the boys with them this time."

Andy spotted Baby. "I wonder how close you are going to get to them today, Norman. You have been so patient with them. You want to get them to eat out of your hand."

"Bill told us to take it slowly," Norman said, "and it can be a very slow process. This is the closest I have been to a herd of wild horses in the open."

We each went to our special man to get our treat. Salty said, as I came to him, "Hello my sweet. Have you missed me? I have missed you. We are going to be great friends." He held out his hand and I took the apple he offered.

Blaze and Chief cautiously moved towards Norman who had an apple in each hand. He stood very still talking softly. "Come on, boys, I won't hurt you. I admit I don't know how I will be able to keep you and your father but we will see."

Quietly, so as not to frighten off the pair of stallions, he almost whispered, "Hey guys, look at this. They finally took the apple. What a treat! To have two wild stallions each take an apple out of my hand is incredible. This I will remember for the rest of my life."

Blaze and Chief were surprised by the sweet good taste of the apple. "The girls were right," Chief mumbled while chewing the remains of his apple.

"Yes, they sure were," Blaze said. "We should have done this sooner."

Baby was with Andy and he just put his hand on Baby's forehead. Baby pulled his head back sharply but since there was no pain he sniffed Andy's hand. *Interesting odour*, he thought. He put his nose in Andy's hand again while Andy simply stood still.

Willful had been left ground-reined and he

wandered over to where I was with Salty and whinnied. "Are you Angel? I recognise Rosie and Star, so you have to be Angel."

"Yes, Father," I said. "I'm Angel. What is it like to live on the ranch?"

"It is different than living here," Willful said. "You always have a man to look after you. I think in time you all will be coming to the ranch."

"Oh, Father," I said, "do you really think so? I have become very fond of the man who feeds me. Would he look after me?"

"Yes, my dear," Willful said, "more than likely." He heard a whistle. "My man is calling me so I have to go now. See you soon."

During this time, Andy said, "I think it is time to leave our Wild Ones for today." He pulled his hand back a little too fast and Rosie took off. "Oh darn, I hope I haven't scared her off. I don't want to start at the beginning again."

125

Rosie ran a short distance then realised no one was chasing her. "Angel, come here please."

"In a minute," I said. "I am enjoying the attention the man is giving me." Salty had not moved while Willful and I were talking. "I have let him touch me after sniffing his hand. It is gentle and comforting in some way."

"Angel, please."

"All right, I am coming. The men were leaving anyway."

"Good-bye for now, my sweet," Salty said as I went over to where Rosie was.

"What is it?" I asked her.

"I got scared when the man moved his hand too fast," Rosie said. "I have to talk to you. I saw you let the man touch you. I wanted to feel that too but he moved so fast. Tell me what it felt like."

"It feels good. There is no discomfort at all," I

told her. "Next time sniff his hand. It is a strange odour but you get used to it."

Many of the others started eating the hay and grain the men had left. Without it many of us would have starved. When there was only six or seven of us there was enough dry grass under the snow but with a big band of hungry, pregnant mares there just was not enough.

"Lady, Lady," I called. "Come and get something to eat."

"Not today, little one," she said. "I can't make it up there now. Maybe later."

I took a mouthful to her then come back for another. I did this a few times but it wasn't enough. *She is getting weaker*, I thought.

"Blaze," I called, "do you think we can get the men to come to her next time? She is too weak to run away."

"Chief and I will talk it over, Angel, and maybe we can do something."

Chapter 16

On the way back to the ranch it started to snow again. Norman said, "It is a good thing we went up to the horses today because we may not have made it tomorrow."

Bill said to the rest of the men, "The Wild Ones are being gentled and don't even know it."

Salty said, "We may be able to ride them come spring. My Sweetie Pie let me touch her. I have to come up with a better name for such a beautiful mare. Any suggestions guys?"

"When have you had such a spirited young lady?" Bob said.

"You said it, Bob," Salty said. "That's what

I will call her, Spirit Lady. She has more spirit than any other horse I've ever seen."

They just entered the ranch yard when the snow became a whiteout. They took the horses and wagon into the barn and brushed them down and put warm blankets over them then went in for the dinner that Cookie had made.

"Andy, Bill," Norman said. "Come in and have dinner with me. I want to talk to you."

"Okay, Boss," they answered.

"After I change into some dry clothes," Andy added.

"Me, too," Bill said.

After they took off their wet outer clothes and changed into clean shirts and pants they went back to the house. Andy knocked before entering. "Every time I come in the house I feel Sophie's presence. I wonder if Norman still feels it, too."

Norman came down the stairs and invited

Bill and Andy in. "Welcome, gentlemen," he said. "A drink to warm your innards before we go into dinner?"

"Coffee for me," Bill said.

"Make that two," Andy agreed.

"Two coffees coming up," Norman said.

In the den, Andy asked, "What is it that you wanted to talk about or should we wait until after dinner?"

"Well," said Norman, "I'm not really sure how to put what I want to suggest."

"Well, Boss," Andy said, "just say it. We will figure it out later."

"Okay, here goes," Norman said. "I want to keep the boys and Willful but I can't figure out how to do that with the three of them being stallions. I could geld the boys or Willful but I don't want to do that. Do either of you have any ideas?"

"Well, Boss," Andy said, "that is the only way I can see of keeping the three of them together."

"Wait a minute," Bill said. "Look at the way Beauty and Willful get along. It is unusual, I know, but we've seen it. There is no animosity between them. We can see after we get the herd to the ranch, how they act together. The boys may be satisfied with their own mares and Willful may be satisfied with the ranch mares. I'll be taking Beauty with me when I go. You said I could have him so he will have his own, too."

"What about that other stallion?" Andy asked. "For some strange reason he does not seem to be anything but a follower not wanting anything to do with the mares."

"That is strange," Norman said. "I have only seen geldings do that. I wish the band could talk to us then we may understand what is going on. They seem to communicate with each other."

After dinner Andy and Bill walked back

to the bunkhouse in the deepening snow. "Bill," Andy said, "tell me what you felt in the house. I always feel as if Sophie is there and I should ask how she is."

"I can't say I felt anything," Bill said, "but then, I didn't know her as well as you did. Well, maybe I did but only for that summer I gentled that horse for her."

"She was a wonderful woman," Andy said. "She would have made a great mother. It is too bad she died so young."

When they reached the bunkhouse they said goodnight and went to their own rooms.

After the snow stopped the men decided that someone should go out to see how the wild horses managed through the blizzard.

Norman took the wagon with Andy and Bill. It was slow going and took twice as long as usual but they made it. As they came over the rise they saw the band coming towards them. Blaze and Chief lead the way this time.

As Salty and Bob started to unload the sleigh, Norman called, "Hi boys. Come, I have your apples." To his surprise they just sniffed the apple and backed away, just out of reach. They repeated this a few times.

Bill said, "Boss, as strange as this may seem, it looks as if they want you to follow them. They want the apple but it is more important at the moment that you follow them."

"This is very strange," Norman said. "What do you think I should do? Could they be leading me into a trap?"

"Norman," Bill said, "that is ridiculous. They don't think like that. That is a human thought. Go with them. We will watch for any funny stuff."

"Okay, boys," Norman said. "Lead the way."

Blaze and Chief headed to where Lady lay under the tree on top of Sophie's grave.

"What have we here?" Norman asked. "You do not look well at all, girl. Andy, Bill, come here quick."

"What is it, Boss?"

"A very sick mare," Norman said.

"You think the stallions led you to her on purpose?" Andy asked.

"Yes," Norman said, "I do believe they want us to take her to the ranch and care for her."

"I am not sure she could walk that far," Bill said, as he bent over Lady and touched her. "This is strange," he said, "she should be cold but is quite warm. I am not sure we can get her up but we can try and maybe we can put her in the sleigh."

"Maybe with the stallions help and one of the sides as a ramp it could work," Norman said thoughtfully.

"How are we going to get the stallions to help us?" Andy asked.

"Well, they led me to her," Norman replied. "Now it is up to us to convey to them what we want. Andy, go bring the sleigh to within a couple of feet then we will see."

While Andy went to get the sleigh, Bill said, "Boss, look at this. You were right. The boys and Spirit Lady are trying to get her to stand."

I nudged her and pleaded with her, "Lady, please get up. Lady, get up."

Blaze was a little more direct then I was. "Lady, up on you feet. You don't have far to go. We're trying to help you. GET UP NOW!

"I don't want your help," Lady said, "What are the men doing here?"

"They are going to take you to the ranch to look after you so you can get well and continue to be our special lady," Chief said.

Finally, she gave in and we got her to her feet

just as Andy brought the sleigh and put one of the sides down as a ramp.

"Well, we will see," Norman said. "They got her up now to see if they can guide her into the wagon."

With Blaze on one side and Chief on the other they guided Lady to the ramp and almost pushed her up it. It was now up to the men to get her on the sleigh and put the side back on. When Lady was on the sleigh she leaned heavily against the side and Bill climbed in with her. She had never had a man touch her but the touch of this man seemed to be comforting.

"Okay, lets go," he said, as Andy and Norman got into the sleigh and they started to move out of the valley. Behind them, they heard the two stallions whinny.

Bill ran his hands over the blond-covered

bones and said, "Well, girl, you really have those boys in your back pocket. We will have to take good care of you." He looked behind him and saw one of the boys was following. "Boss," he said, "look behind us. We have a guard for this girl."

"Well, I'll be," Norman said. "He may follow us all the way to the ranch."

Chief followed at a distance until he was sure the men were going to care for her then he returned to the band. "Blaze," he said, as he came up to where we are eating. "The men have taken her to the ranch. I followed them up to the fence."

"I hope they will be good to her," I said. "The men seem to be very gentle."

"Maybe I should go to the ranch to check on her," Blaze said.

"Don't be foolish," I said. "Just because you

made it once doesn't mean you can do it again."

"Well, I'm going," Blaze replied. "She was a big help to us when we joined her band. Without her we wouldn't be where we are."

"You are right," Chief said. "But I am the one to go this time."

"Can you jump fences?" Blaze asked him. "If you can, yes, you can go but you have to be careful."

"I enjoy jumping but have never jumped a fence," Chief said. "I'll be back before you know I am gone. Rosie, want to come?"

"No way!" Rosie replied. "You be careful."

"Bye, guys," Chief said, as he trotted through the snow.

"Chief!" Rosie called. "Wait, I'll come. I cannot let you go alone. You mean too much to me. I will go as far as the first fence llike Angel did."

"You two be careful," I called after them.

Off on their own, Chief and Rosie were a little scared but each too proud to let on to the other.

So they talked about their lives, the snow and Lady — anything to keep their minds off of what they were really feeling. FEAR! Finally, they got to the first fence.

"You wait here for me," Chief said. "I'll be back as soon as I find out anything."

"I can't. Chief, I can't stay here," Rosie said. "I am too afraid to stay alone. I want to come with you. Please."

"All right but you have to do exactly as I say or I will make you go home."

"I will. I will do anything you say. Just don't make me go home alone."

"Okay, up and over that fence. Let me see you do it."

Up and over Rosie went and then Chief took a run and up and over he went, too.

"Wow, that was great," Rosie said. "I didn't know I liked jumping."

When they got to the ranch yard they saw Lady being taken into the barn with Willful and

Beauty on either side of her.

Norman had gone to the house to phone his vet, Dr. George Jamison.

"Hi, George," he said. "I have a very sick horse here. Could you come and look at her? I think she is undernourished and possibly has pneumonia."

"Which one is it?" George asked. "You look after your animals too well to have an undernourished horse."

"It isn't exactly my horse," Norman said. "It is a long story and I'll tell you when you get here."

"Okay, Norman. I will be right there," the vet said.

When Norman came out of the house he saw Chief and Rosie. "Well, hello, you two. Came to see how the mare is, did you? Well, she is in the barn. Want to come in and see her?"

He went over to Chief and put his hand on his shoulder and gently led him into the barn. He called Bob. "Come and get your horse. She came to see the mare. We may get them into the barn and maybe put a neckerchief around their necks."

Bob came up to Rosie and held out his hand and was rewarded when Rosie took the apple he had in it. She followed him into the barn where Norman had led Chief.

"How is she?" Norman asked Bill, who had stayed with Lady.

"She is very undernourished and is having trouble breathing," Bill answered. "Well, look what you two have. How did you get them to come in here?"

"That is a good question," Norman answered as he put his arm around Chief's neck. "Bill, do you think I can get the kerchief around his neck or would it be in his way when he went back to the herd?"

"I think you can try," Bill said. "And no, it shouldn't be in his way if it is tight enough not to get caught in something but not tight enough to bother him."

"Can I try too with, Rose?" Bob asked excitedly, "She is so red I can't think of a better name for her."

"Yeah, you can try too," Bill said, "but remember, not too tight but tight enough not to get in their way."

"Hi, Father, Cheekie," Chief said. "Will you look after Lady? She was a great help to us when we joined her band. Now it is up to us to look after her. That is why we let the men take her."

"Yes, son I will help look after her," Willful said. "I think that is why the men brought Cheekie and me into the barn with her."

Hearing a noise, Rosie and Chief wanted to run but were worried about Lady.

"Norman, are you in here?" the vet called as he came in the barn. He saw Chief and Rosie and asked, "Who are these two? I haven't seen them before. Where did you get them? Where is the sick mare?"

"Here I am, in the last stall," Norman called. "If I tell you who these two are you won't believe me."

"Try," George said, "while I look at...my, my, this is a sick horse. How did she get like this? I am not sure if I can help her. It might be better to put her out of her misery. I will do what I can. If she makes it through the night she will make it. Help me get her up. We will need a sling to keep her on her feet. Warm mash and plenty of blankets."

Chief and Rosie watched closely. Who was this new man and why was he so close to Lady? They went to push him away when Norman and Bob stopped them.

"It's okay, old boy," Norman said as he rubbed Chief's neck. "This is the doctor. He is going to look after her. Let's go outside so he can do his job. Bob, bring Rose out, too."

Chief was about to resist but Willful calmed him, "I will be here, son. You go with the man. I trust him."

"Okay, Father, if you promise to stay with her," Chief said.

"Father," Rosie added, "take good care of her. She is like a mother to us." Bob led her out.

"Did you hear that?" Bob asked Norman. Those horses were communicating. I don't think these two would have left her if Willful hadn't convinced them to come with us. We could have had a lot of trouble. Did you see the way they were going to attack George?"

"This is an unusual band of wild horses, that is for sure," Norman said. "How am I going to explain this to George?"

"I have no idea," Bob said. "Just tell him the truth. We captured Willful a few years ago and now we are gentling his sons and daughters.

"Yeah, sure!" Norman said, "If I told you that, would you believe me? I know I wouldn't if I hadn't seen it with my own eyes. Besides how do we explain that the patient is a wild mare who has possibly never encountered men in her life before?"

145

"Quit with the unanswerable questions," Bob said.

"Boss," Andy said as he came out of the barn, "we have her standing and the breathing is a little better. Doc said to make sure she has warm mash and water every couple of hours until he comes back in the morning. If she is still alive then, she will be okay."

Bill came out behind him and said, "If I hadn't seen this for myself I would have never believed what just happened in that barn. I am used to wild horses but this is a very strange bunch."

"That is what we have been discussing out here, too," Bob said.

Just then George came out of the barn. "Okay guys, let me in on what just happened in there. Those two almost knocked me over before you brought them outside. Can anyone tell me why?"

"Um, well, you see, George," Norman stammered. "Well, it is this way."

"George," Bill intruded, "you know I am a wild horse trainer. Well, the horse you were treating is a wild mare. These two are in her band. We had been taking food to them all winter. In doing that they have begun to trust us and we are gentling them. This black and grey one is one of the leaders of the band. This other one is one of the band mares. They came to check on how we treated her."

"Get off it. This is too wild to believe. Wild horses do not come into a ranch yard, let alone a barn. Now tell me the real story."

"This is the truth, George," Bob, Norman and Andy all said together. "There is no other truth."

"Besides, that isn't all," Norman said. "There is another black and grey stallion with this band, too. They are leaders together."

"Haven't you heard of the band with two

stallions as leaders?" Bill asked.

"Yeah," George said, "I have heard of this band of horses but thought it was some kind of fairy tale. No two stallions would be co-leaders of a wild band of horses. There would be murder."

"Well, if you have time tomorrow when you come back, we will show you," Andy said.

"Okay," George said, with a gleam of doubt in his eyes, "I will make time to go with you anywhere to see this phenomenon."

The men did not realise that while they were talking Chief and Rosie have left. George, asked, "Where are the two that you brought out?"

"Gone back to the herd I suppose," Andy said. "To let the others know that we have done as they wanted."

"And what would that be?" George asked. "No, don't tell me. I think I know what you are going to say. They wanted you to get help for this mare and now that you have they are satisfied. Baa, humbug!"

During the night everyone took turns looking after Lady. Her breathing got much better and she wasn't so hot to the touch.

"Looks as if she just might make it," Salty said to Bob, who had just come in for the next shift, as dawn peeked over the ridge.

"Oh, good," Bob replied. "Now we have the problem of what to do with a wild old mare who may be too old to gentle?"

"That isn't for us to decide," Salty said as he went out of the barn.

As Bob settled into the hay he heard a strange whinny.

"Where am I?" Lady asked. "How did I get here? Who are you?" She looked at Willful then at Beauty.

"I am your leader's father," Willful replied. "You got here on the men's wagon. My sons led the men to you so they could save you. You were dying. They wanted to save your life and that was the only way they could think of doing it"

"I am their brother," Beauty answered. "You are safe here with us."

Bob listened and wondered what was being said between the three horses. "I wish I could understand what you are saying, boys, but I hope you told the old girl that she is safe here for as long as she wants. Hey, that is a good name for you, Old Girl."

Chapter 17

When Chief and Rosie got back to the valley they told us what they had seen.

Star asked, "You really went into where she was with men in there with her?"

Chief answered, "We had to. That was where they had taken her."

Rosie added, "Father and Cheekie were with her so we left her in good hands."

"Another man came in after and went into where she was being kept," Chief said. "We were going to chase him away but were taken outside by our men."

"Then when the new man came out we took our chance to escape," Rosie added.

Blaze, had been looking at something around

Chief and Rosie's neck, said, "What is that around your neck, Chief? Rosie has one, too."

"I don't know," Chief said. "The man put his arm around my neck and it seemed to remain there even after we left the ranch."

"Mine, too," Rosie said.

Blaze went over to sniff the kerchief and tried to get it to come off but it was secure. He then tried to get Rosie's off but it was also secure.

"Does it hurt?" I ask and nuzzled Rosie.

"No," Rosie answered. "It doesn't hurt at all. In fact it feels fine."

We felt much better now that the men were looking after Lady. The next morning as we finished our morning drink we heard the sound of horses coming. We still had food but we went to meet them anyway as we enjoyed our contact with them. Blaze and Chief eagerly went to Norman now.

George recognised Chief and was surprised that this was the same horse that could and would have killed him yesterday. With Norman he was almost as gentle as a domesticated horse.

"Wow!" he said. "You are right. If I hadn't seen this for myself I would have never believed it. How did you do this?"

Norman replied, as he gave Blaze and Chief each a carrot, "I really don't know for sure. Willful is their father and Beauty is their brother. They must have been here in the valley when we captured the band and left after Beauty came over the ridge. They must have come back because they knew their valley was safe. Now, having fed them all winter, they have come to trust us and come to us for treats. The mares came first, now the stallions are coming just as willingly."

Bill, on Beauty, added, "We assume they defeated the white stallion and took over together and the palomino helped or taught them how to lead. Now they are caring for her. I am sure if Bob and Norman hadn't taken them out yesterday they would have attacked you. They trusted their father and brother to care for her."

"Norman," George said, "do you think I could have one of the stallions?"

"That is up to the horse," Norman replied. "They have picked us. We have not picked them."

"How do I go about it?" George asked. "This would be the first time I've tried to tame a wild horse."

"I'll show you," Bill said. "First pick the one you want then do exactly what I tell you."

"I would like the one that tried to kill me." George said.

"That is a good choice," Norman said. "The one I almost got a halter on. I have the father and the other one. I have to come up with a name for you, don't I?" he said to Blaze.

Norman gave George an apple and led the black over to him. "George, take the apple and hold it in your hand. Do not move."

Chief followed Norman because he wanted the apple then he stopped short. "That is the man who was in the barn with Lady," he whinnied to Blaze and me.

"Do not move!" Bill whispered. "He wants the apple but he just realised who you are."

"Okay," George said, "but for how long? This is the wild stallion that would have killed me yesterday. He looks as if he isn't sure whether or not to do it now."

Norman added, "Until he makes up his mind whether he wants the apple or he leaves, he doesn't know if he can trust you. Besides, I don't think he will attack you."

Chief walked back to where Norman had gone to pat Blaze and nuzzled his hand. "Well, he has made up his mind, George. You may have to pick another or take the time we did with them all winter."

Bill said, "It looks like it isn't so much the apple but the attachment between Norman and the boys."

"It doesn't look as if either of the blacks are going to leave Norman now," Andy said.

Baby came from the lake where he had been drinking.

"What about this one, Bill?" George asked.

"He hasn't made a connection with any of us, really."

George held out his hand with the apple

in it towards Baby who took it and munched it with relish.

Bob and Norman took the kerchiefs off Chief's and Rosie's necks and slipped a halter on each. Norman put his arm around Blaze's neck with the kerchief in his hand and gently tied the ends. At this time, Salty put a scarf around my neck. Star had one, too. The men remounted and head back for the ranch.

When they reach the ranch, George checked on his patient again. She had become agitated and was trying to kick the sides of the stall but was still too weak. "Well, Goldie," he said, "you must be feeling a whole lot better. Can I come in and check on you before I let you out?"

Norman and Bill thought it was a good idea to bring Willful and Beauty into the barn.

157

When Lady saw them she calmed right down. "Where have you been?" she asked. "I got scared here by myself."

"We went to the band," Willful said to her. "Blaze, Chief and the rest told me to tell you they miss you and want you back as soon as you are well. Now, calm down. We are back to care for you."

George, who was about to enter the stall, stopped and watched the exchange between the three horses. Suddenly, the mare calmed down. He entered the stall and did a quick exam. "I think we can let her out tomorrow. What calmed her down so fast? Was it bringing Willful and Beauty in the barn?"

"That's right," Norman said. "I told you this was a very strange band of wild horses. Thanks George. Send me the bill. We are going back up there in about five days with more food. You are welcome to join us if you like and have the time."

"Thanks, Norman. I would like to come again. That little horse and I are going to be good friends."

Five days later, George went out with the men to the herd and over the next month got to know Baby.

Chapter 18

We all wore halters now.

The winter had been hard and cold. Records were set for lowest temperatures. Our band would not have survived until spring if not for the loads of hay and grain. The men had to break the ice every time they came. By the time the weather warmed, the ice melted and the snow receded, the men had us accepting being led by reins attached to the halters. We were led slowly onto the ranch so the babies and yearlings that were with us could be claimed as Circle Bar X horses.

"We are sure lucky, Boss," Andy said to Norman. "If it hadn't been for Willful, we would never have had this healthy good-looking band of mares."

"Well," Norman said, "we can thank the boys for that, too. If they had not brought them back to White Buffalo Valley we would not have had them either."

"Yes," Bob said. "That is right. Those boys of yours are to be thanked for bringing us this wonderful herd. Are we going to sell the yearlings?"

"Yes, after they are broken we will sell them to people we know will look after them well," Norman said.

Salty, who led Angel into the yard asked, "Bill may have a big job in front of him with all these wild ones to gentle."

"Boss," Andy said, "I just had a wonderful idea. Why don't we advertise for anyone who wants to come and learn how to gentle his or her own wild colt or mare? We can charge a nominal fee for bed and breakfast then they can do it themselves. Get to know their horse on an even deeper level."

"We would have to see how Bill feels about giving lessons to novices but that would be a great idea. Sophie wanted to do that when she was alive. By the way, I have come up with names for the boys. The one who seems to be the lead stallion will be Black Gold and the other Quick Silver."

"Boss," Salty asked, "what are we going to do with three studs?"

"Well, I have decided to let the boys stay in White Buffalo Valley and Willful will be here on the ranch. Beauty will be with Bill and go with him or be here when Bill is here. It is up to Bill what he does with him."

We were all Circle Bar X horses and happy to

be home. Lady was well and learned how to accept men, too. She deserved a peaceful retirement with no worries about young horses that do not know anything. We mares all had healthy colts or fillies and make good mothers with Lady's help. She is a wonderful grandmother.

The End

Made in the USA
Charleston, SC
12 October 2013